Dear Parents:

Congratulations! Your child is taking the first steps on an exciting journey. The destination? Independent reading!

STEP INTO READING® will help your child get there. The program offers five steps to reading success. Each step includes fun stories and colorful art or photographs. In addition to original fiction and books with favorite characters, there are Step into Reading Non-Fiction Readers, Phonics Readers and Boxed Sets, Sticker Readers, and Comic Readers—a complete literacy program with something to interest every child.

Learning to Read, Step by Step!

Ready to Read   Preschool–Kindergarten
• big type and easy words • rhyme and rhythm • picture clues
For children who know the alphabet and are eager to begin reading.

Reading with Help   Preschool–Grade 1
• basic vocabulary • short sentences • simple stories
For children who recognize familiar words and sound out new words with help.

Reading on Your Own   Grades 1–3
• engaging characters • easy-to-follow plots • popular topics
For children who are ready to read on their own.

Reading Paragraphs   Grades 2–3
• challenging vocabulary • short paragraphs • exciting stories
For newly independent readers who read simple sentences with confidence.

Ready for Chapters   Grades 2–4
• chapters • longer paragraphs • full-color art
For children who want to take the plunge into chapter books but still like colorful pictures.

STEP INTO READING® is designed to give every child a successful reading experience. The grade levels are only guides; children will progress through the steps at their own speed, developing confidence in their reading.

Remember, a lifetime love of reading starts with a single step!

Visit us on the Web!
StepIntoReading.com
randomhousekids.com

Educators and librarians, for a variety of teaching tools, visit us at RHTeachersLibrarians.com

ISBN 978-0-553-52314-0 (trade) — ISBN 978-0-553-52315-7 (lib. bdg.)

Printed in the United States of America 10 9 8 7 6 5 4 3 2 1

STEP INTO READING®

STEP 1

READY TO READ

nickelodeon

Wallykazam!

The Cake Monster

by Jennifer Liberts
based on the episode by Scott Gray
illustrated by David VanTuyle

Random House 🏠 New York

It is Ogre Doug's birthday!

He is having a party.

There are fun games!

It is time
for birthday cake!
Wally and Libby
bring out
Ogre Doug's cake.

Oh, no!
The Cake Monster
smells the cake.

The Cake Monster wants the cake!

Wally holds up

his magic stick.

It rains french fries!
The Cake Monster
does not want fries.
He wants cake!

Wally uses his
magic stick.
He frosts the tree.

The Cake Monster
does not want frosting.
He only wants cake!

I LOVE
CAKE

Wally holds up
his magic stick.
He gives
the Cake Monster
feathers!

Feathers do not stop
the Cake Monster.
He still wants cake!

Wally hides the cake
in a fort.
Ogre Doug
takes a bite.

No!

The Cake Monster
takes the cake!

Ogre Doug is sad.
Wally and Norville
will get the cake!

Wally and Norville
fly fast.
They get the cake back!

The Cake Monster
is sad.

It is his birthday, too.

The Cake Monster
says he is sorry.
Wally asks him
to join the party.

Ogre Doug eats
his birthday cake.
The Cake Monster
makes new friends!